D0710812

# The
# Great Galaxy
# Goof

# Books by Robert Elmer

ASTROKIDS

> #1 / *The Great Galaxy Goof*
> #2 / *The Zero-G Headache*

PROMISE OF ZION

> #1 / *Promise Breaker*
> #2 / *Peace Rebel*
> #3 / *Refugee Treasure*

ADVENTURES DOWN UNDER

> #1 / *Escape to Murray River*
> #2 / *Captive at Kangaroo Springs*
> #3 / *Rescue at Boomerang Bend*
> #4 / *Dingo Creek Challenge*
> #5 / *Race to Wallaby Bay*
> #6 / *Firestorm at Kookaburra Station*
> #7 / *Koala Beach Outbreak*
> #8 / *Panic at Emu Flat*

THE YOUNG UNDERGROUND

> #1 / *A Way Through the Sea*
> #2 / *Beyond the River*
> #3 / *Into the Flames*
> #4 / *Far From the Storm*
> #5 / *Chasing the Wind*
> #6 / *A Light in the Castle*
> #7 / *Follow the Star*
> #8 / *Touch the Sky*

# ROBERT ELMER

## AstroKids

# The Great Galaxy Goof

BETHANY BACKYARD®
www.bethanyhouse.com

*The Great Galaxy Goof*
ASTROKIDS
Copyright © 2000
Robert Elmer

Cover and text illustrations by Paul Turnbaugh
Cover design by Lookout Design Group, Inc.

Scripture quotations are from the *International Children's Bible, New Century Version,* copyright © 1986, 1988 by Word Publishing, Dallas, Texas 75039. Used by permission.

All rights reserved. No part of this publication may be reproduced, stored in a retrieval system, or transmitted in any form or by any means—electronic, mechanical, photocopying, recording, or otherwise—without the prior written permission of the publisher and copyright owners.

Published by Bethany House Publishers
A Ministry of Bethany Fellowship International
11400 Hampshire Avenue South
Minneapolis, Minnesota 55438
www.bethanyhouse.com

Printed in the United States of America by
Bethany Press International, Minneapolis, Minnesota 55438

**Library of Congress Cataloging-in-Publication Data**

Elmer, Robert.
    The great galaxy goof / by Robert Elmer.
        p. cm. — (AstroKids ; 1)
    Summary: Buzz Bright, a newcomer to CLEO-7, the new space station orbiting the moon, finds his Christian principles tested by an unfriendly prankster. Includes a history of space stations and instructions for decoding a secret message.
    ISBN 0-7642-2356-9 (pbk.)
    [1. Space stations—Fiction. 2. Christian life—Fiction. 3. Science fiction.] I. Title.
    PZ7.E4794 Gr 2000
    [Fic]—dc21

                                                   00-009928

To Steve H. . . .

Robert

Freckles

**ROBERT ELMER** is an Earth-based author who writes for life-forms all over the solar system. He was born the year after the first *Sputnik* satellite was launched, and grew up while Russia and the United States were racing to put a man on the moon. *Why not a boy on the moon?* he wanted to know. Today, Robert lives with his wife, Ronda, their three kids, and a non-computerized dog friend. Their house is about ninety-three million miles from the sun.

# Contents

✳ ✳ ✳

# MEET THE
# AstroKids

## Lamar "Buzz" Bright

Show the way, Buzz! The leader of the AstroKids always has a great plan. He also loves Jupiter ice cream.

## Daphne "DeeBee" Ortiz

DeeBee's the brains of the bunch—she can build or fix almost anything. But, suffering satellites, don't tell her she's a "GEEN-ius"!

## Theodore "Tag" Ortiz

Yeah, DeeBee's little brother, Tag, always tags along. Count on him to say something silly at just the wrong time. He's in orbit.

## Kumiko "Miko" Sato

Everybody likes Miko the stowaway. They just don't know how she got to be a karate master, or how she knows so much about space shuttles.

## Vladimir "Mir" Chekhov

So his dad's the station commander and Mir usually gets his way? Give him a break! He's trying. And whatever he did, it was probably just a joke.

# 1 Tag, You're It

I knew something was strange the first time I heard that noise in the space-shuttle kitchen.

Like a gasp.

I was going to punch in the data code for a snack. Press 2-0-0-7 for Astro-cheesies. I had that code memorized.

But then I heard it again. Back in the corner, right behind the digital food copier. (That's what makes meals. I'll explain later.)

Anyway, it was a human gasp, not a machine gasp.

"Hello?" I checked the little garbage chute door. "Anyone here?"

*Whoosh!* It almost sucked my hand into space. I slammed the door.

That's when I felt kind of silly.

*Come on,* I told myself. *You're just hearing things.*

To tell you the truth, I didn't really want to meet anyone crawling out of the garbage chute. Or out from inside the wall. I'd heard too many scary alien stories. *The Three-Eyed Creature of the Cargo Area,* that sort of thing.

So I decided the noise was a shuttle noise. And the shuttle was just doing what shuttles do. Flying from Earth to the space stations, to the moon colony, and back again. Shuttles make noises, right?

Right. Something clicked over my head. Something else beeped. A whoosh of air. Normal shuttle noises.

"Hey!" A little kid floating upside down back by my seat yelled and waved at me. "You've got to see this. It's *CLEO-7!*"

He was staring out my window and flapping his hands like a bird. I think he was excited to see the space station.

*Our* space station.

"Where? Really?" I forgot about the noise, and about being hungry. I settled for a soda disk.

QUESTION 01:
What's a soda disk, anyway?

ANSWER 01:
You've never heard of a soda disk? Wow!
It's like a whole can of soda pop squeezed
into the size of an Oreo cookie. They're awesome.

QUESTION 02:
Wait a minute. A cookie?

ANSWER 02:
The *size* of a smallish cookie. You stuff it in
your mouth, and the soda comes out slowly.
But once you put it in your mouth, you have
to keep it there, or it makes a mess. It's still
not perfect. But what do you expect? It's
only 2175.

Anyway, I flipped over backward in midair.
Then I pushed off from the wall. I love being
weightless, even more than playing laser tag. Even

more than flying back on Earth. Weightlessness is the best! I slipped the cola soda disk in my pocket and glided back to my seat.

"Did you know it was so big?" asked the kid. He made a little grease smudge where he pressed his nose against the round space shuttle window. "It looks like a huge *regrub-mah*."

"What's that?" I didn't know what a *regrub-mah* was. Maybe it was some kind of moon word.

"*Hamburger*, silly. Only spelled backward."

Oh. I smiled at the lame joke and peeked out at the huge double-decker hamburger myself. Like a city in the sky, with lights flashing all around. I caught my breath at the sight.

Three rows back, a girl stood up. She pointed my way.

"Tag, you come back here," said the girl. "You're bothering people again."

I looked around. I wasn't Tag. She wasn't pointing at me, but at the little guy next to me.

"No, it's okay," I answered. "He's all right."

Okay, he *was* a bit of a pain. He was making me dizzy, floating upside down next to my head. But you could tell he didn't mean anything by it.

Tag didn't listen to her.

"Tag, did you hear me?" She pulled away from her spot with a *ri-ip* of Velcro. Everybody was stuck to their seats that way—unless they wanted to go spinning around the inside of the shuttle. And twenty-five spinning people would not be good. They would probably be sick.

I decided the girl must be Tag's older sister. I could tell from her face. She was about my age, but white instead of black like me, with long brown hair.

She was sure acting bossy. And she wasn't very happy with Tag. I could tell *that* from her face.

"Tag, did you hear me?" she tried again. She started toward us. But a red light on her wrist interface blinked just then.

(I would explain what an interface is. But you'll get it by reading what happens next.)

Anyway, I could see a tiny 3-D head projected right above her wristwatch. Well, it wasn't actually a wristwatch. It *looked* like a wristwatch. But it was really an interface.

And even though a floating head sounds strange, it was great! The 3-D picture of a head was about as big as your fist. You could see all around it, like a doll's head. The eyes, the ears, hair, everything. This man's head was talking, just like you would talk to someone if you were face-to-face. That's why they call it an interface.

But the tone of the man's voice worried me. I could tell something was wrong.

Way wrong.

## 2 GEEN-ius ✳ ✳ ✳

"Incoming shuttle," said the talking head floating above the girl's interface. "You'll have to hold where you are. The shuttle bay doors are . . . uh . . . stuck."

*Welcome to* CLEO-7, I thought. *The garage doors don't even work.*

The girl didn't answer right away. Instead, she touched the edge of her wrist screen and up jumped another face. Or head, I mean. He was pretty nervous-looking, too. I could almost see the sweat running down his forehead.

"We're working on it," this face said. "I don't know what happened."

"I thought the station was new." I should have kept my mouth shut.

The girl didn't look at me as she walked up. She

didn't float. She kept her Velcro boots stuck tightly to the floor.

"New stations always have a few bugs," she said.

I was hoping she meant bugs, as in things wrong with computer programs. That kind of bug. Not stinky real bugs with a hundred legs and antennae. Real bugs are okay—just not in my space station.

She touched the screen again. She surfed between five, maybe ten, channels. All of them had nervous people on them, people trying to fix the doors. After all, we wanted to land in the station, not crash into it.

"How do you get all those channels?" I asked her. "I have only two."

She grinned and looked down. Was it some kind of secret?

"Here, let me see your interface." She held out her hand.

I pulled it from my wrist and handed it over.

She snapped off the back and traded two parts inside. Little electronic things I don't understand.

Then she turned a knob with her thumbnail. Finally, she popped the cover back on and handed it back. It had taken her about two minutes, tops.

"This'll give you more power," she told me. She grinned again.

"My sister, DeeBee, is a GEEN-ius," said Tag. "Our dad taught her everything. He's the chief solar-tech at the station, and we lived here for three months, but then we visited my aunt and uncle on another station, and now we're coming back, and—"

"Tag! Shh," DeeBee interrupted. "Anyway, Lamar, just be extra careful how you use the interface. It's Lamar, isn't it?"

I nodded and wondered how she knew my name. She *did* look pretty smart. "Yes, but—"

But she wasn't waiting around for me to say "thank you" or "nice view." By that time, big sister DeeBee was talking to another 3-D head. Something about fixing circuits and backup panels. Whatever *that* meant.

"Thanks," I whispered after her as she dragged Tag back to his seat.

I glanced at my wrist. *Be extra careful?* Okay. But I had to test it out.

So I touched the side of my interface, and people popped up one at a time. People from *CLEO*-7. I almost laughed, they seemed so real. Most looked back at me with eyes popping big with surprise.

"Hey—" said one. He looked like he'd just woken up.

I switched channels.

"Now, wait a—" began another. His mouth was full. Lunchtime?

"You, there!" said a third. She put a hand over her face. I think she needed to comb her hair.

I switched channels again before they could ask what I was doing. Sure, they would see my face, too. But it was fun switching channels, the way DeeBee had. Just to see what it was like.

On about the twentieth channel, though, I wasn't quick enough.

It was a kid this time, not an adult. A guy about my age. He was laughing and laughing. Like someone had just told a great joke.

"This is too good," the kid said. "Nobody will ever find out."

I wasn't sure what he meant, or whom he was talking to. Maybe to himself. But he started laughing again. "Ha-ha-ha-ha snort!" Boy, was it funny.

I almost had to start laughing, too, even though I didn't know the joke. Laughing is kind of catchy, you know.

But when I giggled, this guy found out that I had tuned in.

He looked straight at me. "Who are you?" he demanded. His voice had an accent. Russian, maybe?

I froze. The joke was over.

"And what are you doing on my private holo-channel?"

That was "holo," as in a 3-D hologram. Not "hollow," like nothing inside.

"Sorry," I told him. How could I explain? "I didn't mean to spy on you. I was just trying something out. I'm on the shuttle, on my way down to the station."

"That's no excuse." The boy frowned. "My father isn't going to like this. I'll be waiting for you, kid."

"Uh . . . I can explain."

The little head above my interface disappeared. He had hung up on me. And now this angry kid would be waiting for me. *Great.*

"Who were you talking to, Lamar?" My mother slipped back into her seat.

"Oh, just another kid down on the station," I answered. *Who is he, though?*

"See?" Mom smiled. "And you were so worried. You're making friends already, and we're just landing."

Not quite true. Yeah, we were landing soon—if they had fixed the doors. But the guy waiting for me at the station? Well, somehow I didn't think we were going to be best friends.

My dad followed Mom to his seat. He was going to be the new chief of security at *CLEO-7.* "Excited?" he asked.

I nodded. Sure, I was excited. Maybe a little scared, too. Who wouldn't be? It's not every day you move to a huge space station with your family.

But if I knew then what I know now, I would have been a lot less excited. And a lot more scared. A whole lot more scared.

# 3 Call Me Buzz  ✳ ✳ ✳

Just before we landed, Tag and I watched the
station out my window again. He was an okay little
kid. A little squirrelly, but okay, even when he tried
to tell those silly backward jokes. He helped me
keep my mind off the guy who was waiting for me.
The kid from my interface, down on the station.

And what did Tag say—that *CLEO-7* looked
like a double-decker hamburger? Well, kind of.
Only it was covered with a shiny metal skin—tita-
nium, I think.

Of course it was bigger. Way bigger. And the
closer we got, the more awesome it looked. Sort of
like a slow-spinning 3-D hologram game.

Except this was the real thing. That's what was
so different. Even the view on the holo-screens in
the back of each seat was awesome. You would
have thought the same thing if you were there.

"I guess it's big enough to fit ten of my old school buildings inside," I told him. I tried to measure with my hands, but there was no way. "Or maybe twenty. Or thirty."

"How would you drag your old school building all the way up here?" he asked. "*CLEO*-7 is right next to the moon."

Good old Earth *was* a long way behind us. About four hundred thousand kilometers. (A mile is almost twice as long as a kilometer. Okay, five kilometers are about the same as three miles. You can do the arithmetic.)

Anyway, trust me, it's a long way. It was hard to believe this was going to be our new home.

Maybe Tag was thinking about home, too. Wherever that had been. So we didn't say much else for a while. We just oohed and ahhed and watched the huge space station turn.

Two people in space suits were working their way out on the spinning edge of the big burger. They made sparks, like little fireflies back home on Earth. They rode the station around, too. And then they jetted toward the center, on the underside.

"Right there." I pointed. "See those round doors on the flat side, in the middle? That's what they were trying to fix, I think. Those doors go into the big shuttle garage, the shuttle bay . . . whatever you call it. That's where we'll go in."

"I knew that, Lamar."

"Oh, right," I said. "But, listen, only my parents call me Lamar."

"What about everybody else?"

"Buzz. They call me Buzz."

"Buzzzz." Tag smiled. He was missing a front tooth. "Like the bee?"

"No." I'd heard that one before. "Like the famous pioneer astronaut Buzz Aldrin. He was the second man to walk on the moon. July 20, 1969—"

"We haven't studied ancient history yet." The boy held up his finger to stop me. "I just started school."

"Sure. Sorry."

Of course Tag wouldn't know much history yet. And 1969 was more than two hundred years ago. That's a long time.

But I couldn't help remembering what I read.

Ever walk through a field and have burrs stick to your socks? You know, back home on Earth? That's how it is for me whenever I read something. I hold the e-book in my hand and turn on the flat white screen. And if I read something, I can't forget it. Jokes, Bible verses, whatever.

Hearing things is the same way. I remember *everything*. Sometimes it drives me crazy. I'm afraid that when I someday get to be an old geezer—like maybe fifteen or sixteen—my brain's going to be overflowing with stuff I can't forget!

That's exactly why something else was still bothering me. I couldn't forget hearing the sound— the gasp in the shuttle's kitchen. That's why it bothered me even more when I heard it again.

## 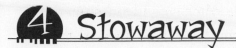 4 Stowaway ✳ ✳ ✳

"See you *retal*." Tag waved at me as he pushed his way out of the shuttle. He meant *later*, of course.

I waved back. I was last in line to get off the ship.

Not just because I didn't want to meet the guy on my wrist interface, you understand. I'm usually not afraid of anybody. But I had this hunch.

"I need to check something," I whispered to my mom. "Be right there."

In a minute, workers would probably be coming to clean things up for the next flight in the morning. I didn't have much time. So I ducked between two rows of seats and pulled up my legs. I tried not to breathe. Everybody else shuffled off. You could hear their slow footsteps, sticking and unsticking from the floor.

I was listening for the noise again. The noise I'd heard when I was looking for a snack in the kitchen. The noise I'd heard again just minutes ago.

This time I was sure.

Well, almost sure.

Actually, I was surprised my mom didn't come back for me. Instead, I heard a wall panel pop off. Someone grunted. You'd grunt, too, if you'd just spent the day in a dark storage cabinet.

Someone was crawling out of a hiding place. I hoped it was no Three-Eyed Creature of the Cargo Area.

Remember that we were still weightless. That's the way it was in the middle of *CLEO-7*—in the hub, where the shuttles landed. We would start to feel gravity once we were inside the station. Artificial gravity, it's called—feels just like being on Earth.

But anyway, I wasn't thinking about gravity just then. I was ready for when the stowaway drifted by. I heard breathing. Then I saw a foot.

"Gotcha!" I said. I grabbed the stowaway from the side. "You're in trouble now."

At first, all I could tell was that the stowaway was small. And that it was probably a girl. She had a short, thick mop of dark black hair. And she knew some good moves.

"Yee!" screamed the stowaway.

Just my luck—I had grabbed a stowaway karate expert.

"Ahh!" She pulled me over her shoulder and flipped me into the ceiling.

That didn't feel very good. My head connected with a control panel. Something beeped and snapped off—from the control panel, not from my head.

"Ow!" I moaned, rubbing the back of my skull.

"Oh dear," said the stowaway. "Are you all right?"

Did she care? I stared for a moment, trying to figure out what was happening. The front of my shirt was wet. Great—she had broken the soda disk in my pocket. Ever poured a soda down your shirt?

"I didn't mean to hurt you," she said. "You just scared me."

"I'm okay." I stared at my karate attacker. Like

DeeBee, she was about the same age as I was. And you could tell her family had once come from Japan.

Anyway, she floated closer to me now. She looked sorry, I think, for slamming me up against the ceiling. Well, she should have. My head still hurt, and my shirt was wet.

I clicked the loose control-panel handle back on. "You shouldn't have done that," I mumbled.

"Lamar?" It was my mom. She was coming back to see what was taking me so long. "Are you coming?"

"Please don't tell," whispered the stowaway. Like a cat, she slipped back to her hiding place.

"Wait a minute," I said. "What are you going to do? Who are you?"

"No. Please, I just . . ."

The look on this girl's face made me want to trust her. She looked at me with big, dark eyes.

I made a nanosecond decision.

"Lamar?" Mom poked her head back into the far end of the shuttle. "People are waiting for us."

"Okay, Mom." I sighed. "Do they know karate?"

"What?"

"Nothing. I'm coming. Just had a little . . . uh . . . accident with a soda disk."

I looked back toward the stowaway, but she was hiding again. I took another deep breath and headed for the exit.

*I know* one *person who's waiting for me,* I thought. Even if he didn't know karate, I didn't want to meet the boy from my wrist interface.

# Warning:
## 5 System Error

*** 

*WHOOSH!*

The double doors slammed shut right behind me. I did a quick jig to keep my foot from being pinched.

"Wow." I looked at our station-drone to see what had happened. "Were they supposed to do that?"

Our guide turned its three buggy camera eyes to study my parents and me. The drone floated about a meter above the floor. It looked sort of like a silver basketball, except with three skinny arms that had grabber claws on the ends. Of course, this station-drone was smarter than most basketballs I knew.

"Presently, we are experiencing minor technical troubles," droned the drone. It didn't have a mouth, but we could hear it fine. "Follow me,

please, and I will show you the rest of the station."
So we did. And here's what we saw.

01—The labs. Where people did experiments.
Everyone was dressed in blue there—even
the light was blue. My dad called them
"blue labs."

02—The repair center. Full of half-built station-
drones, chore-drones, and very cool electronic gizmos. This was where the *techs*
worked. (That's short for technicians.)

03—The gardens. A huge room with a tall ceiling, full of plants and ponds. It reminded
me of Earth.

04—The apartments. Each family got one, and
ours opened up to the gardens. Nice view!
I had my own little—but way cool—room
with a small round window. And not far
from our place we saw two big rooms people could use for meetings and church. Dad
thought he already knew two families who
would go to church with us.

05—The dining center. On one wall were digital

food copiers, rows of tiny key pads, and holo-screens to show 3-D pictures of everything on the menu. People sat at floating round tables and watched the view through two big skylights.

There was a lot more, too, like a health clinic, workshops, exercise rooms, and the security center, where my dad would work . . . but it would all take way too long to describe. (You'll find your way around eventually.)

I didn't see the guy from the interface anywhere, which was good. But sooner or later, I would. I knew that. With only 152 people and 112 drones on *CLEO-7*, you were bound to meet everyone.

Even so, this was the coolest place I had ever seen. By far. Way cooler than even the Mile High Shopping Mall or the Space Flight Museum back home in Seattle.

"The navigation center is there to your right," our station-drone told us, pointing a laser beam at the room on the right. We could see nearly twenty nav-tech people in there, sitting at workstations.

Red light reflected off their faces. A couple of chore-drones buzzed around them.

"Look at their view, Lamar." My mom smiled and pointed to the huge windows. These people could see everything. The stars, incoming shuttles, everything. It was awesome.

"And . . . *hic* . . . over there . . ." began the drone, but for a minute, it couldn't talk, only hiccup. Weird. It had been working fine.

My mom looked at my dad the way she did when it was his turn to fix a circuit. Now, my dad is very smart, but fixing things is not his specialty.

"Walt, maybe we'd better exchange the drone," she whispered. "This one doesn't seem to be working."

"No exchanges or . . . *hic* . . . returns without a receipt," squeaked the station-drone, and it spun around. "To your left is the NavDeck 01 bathroom. And over there—"

The drone pointed its green laser pointer in ten different directions. I started to laugh as it spun faster and faster.

"I am a 61-40 station-drone," squealed the

drone as it whirled. "My purpose . . . oo-la-la . . . is to provide support for the crew of *CLEO*-7. Oh, grooovy, man! Ha-ha-ha-ha SNORT!"

I thought I'd heard that laugh before. But this was no joke. Smoke started to fizz out of the poor drone's seams. I thought maybe it was going to explode.

"I am programmed with three centuries of top 40 musical highlights for your . . . *hic* . . . entertainment."

*What in the world. . . ?*

I tried to grab the thing, but by now it was spinning too fast.

The drone sang about putting your left arm in, and then taking your left arm out. And then putting your right leg in, and taking your right arm out . . . And then there was some kind of hokey, or pokey— I'm not sure.

What a weird old song!

"I'm calling tech support," my dad said. He pressed a button on his interface.

By that time, our drone was stuck on a song about . . . did I hear it right? I thought he was asking, "Oh, wheeere is my hairbrush?" But that couldn't have been right.

Never mind hairbrushes. This drone needed a brain-chip transplant. He was going wacko!

"Oh, wheeere is my—" screamed the drone.

I plugged my ears. Who programmed this thing? Where was the Off switch?

Just when I thought it couldn't get worse, the doors ahead of us started opening and closing to the music. *Swish-swoosh*. The overhead lights blinked with the rhythm. *Blinkity-blink*. A couple of white-shirted techs in the hall stopped and stared, too. One guy tried to tell the others it was just a glitch in the new program.

Some glitch. We needed major help with this thing. So I did a little calling.

"May I help you?" asked the interface tech support person. I stepped back around the corner from the guide-drone. By this time it was spitting green sparks. Cool. I whispered the name I wanted, and a second later Tag's big sister popped up from my interface. She wrinkled her nose at me.

"Oh, hello." She must have remembered me

from the shuttle. "You're Lam—"

"Hi, yeah, it's Buzz Bright. Remember me? I'm on NavDeck 01, and—"

"What's all that noise?" she wanted to know. "Is someone singing?"

"Sort of. But you've got to explain something to me, DeeBee—fast. The drones, the doors, the lights . . . Something very weird is happening on *CLEO-7*."

*WHOOSH! WHOOSH!* I had to duck as two more drones flew by.

# 6 Ha-Ha Whoops ✳ ✳ ✳

*ZING!*

I barely ducked that one. This was no station-drone. This was an attack-drone! And it had plenty of friends just like it. Some were singing more weird songs—something about chewing gum losing its flavor on the bedpost overnight. Others were just bursting into that horrible, annoying laugh as they whizzed by.

Think of dozens of silver basketballs with arms, shooting down the hallways at light speed. They weren't aiming for us, I don't think, just going nutso. And we didn't want to be in their way when that happened.

"Incoming!" shouted DeeBee, and she pulled me to the deck. I was glad she'd made it so quickly.

*ZWAANG!* Another one shot by us, just over our heads.

"Ha-ha-ha-ha SNORT!"

The mag-lev force field that held each drone up in the air made the back of my neck tingle. My buzz-cut hair always stood up, but DeeBee's long hair looked really funny standing up. Ever had that static feeling?

QUESTION 03:

Okay, hold on. You're going to have to explain that one. What is *mag-lev*?

ANSWER 03:

*Mag-lev* is short for *magnetic levitation*. You know what magnets are, and how they push against each other when you put the negative or positive ends together. *Levitation* just means floating. Get it?

So anyway, back to the drones. "What's *with* these crazy things?" I yelled at DeeBee.

"I don't know." DeeBee tried to smooth her hair and got back up. "But we're going to find out."

I was already finding out—about DeeBee Ortiz.

By the way, DeeBee stands for *database*, as in computer. And if DeeBee said she would fix something, I believed her. Remember what she did to my interface?

*ZVOOOP!* Another drone. I danced out of the way and followed DeeBee down the hallway on my knees.

"Why are we going to the hub?" I asked.

She gave me a look, like, *What asteroid are you from?* "Because that's where I think the problem is."

"Are you sure? Why don't we let the adults fix it?" Well, I thought it was a good question. Made sense to me.

DeeBee reached up and punched a code into a key pad on the wall. A door swooshed open in front of us.

"You're new here," she told me.

Obviously. So was just about everyone else.

"You're going to find out that the adults on this station are nice. But they don't listen to us Astro-Kids."

"They don't?"

"Well, sometimes they do. But not always. Anyway, the controls to the drone mag-lev system are here in the hub. And I say somebody's been messing with them."

Okay. I looked at the sign next to the door. Authorized Personnel Only.

"Doesn't that mean 'Keep Out'?"

"I passed the tech test," she told me. "I'm okay to go in."

"Great." I was impressed.

"So are you going to help me fix this, or not?"

Well, sure I would. We were already one step into the big shuttle hangar 02. And from behind one of the two big shuttles . . .

"*Hii-YAH!*"

*Oh no*. This time I knew what to do.

But DeeBee wasn't as quick as I was.

"Watch out for the—" I tried to tell her.

Too late. DeeBee got an elbow in the ear. That had to hurt.

But this time it was two against one. And even Miss Karate Stowaway couldn't get past both

DeeBee *and* me. We held her down before she could get away.

"So *you're* the one!" cried DeeBee.

Case solved, right?

But I had to feel bad for the stowaway—as if I was being cruel or something. She flashed me a look. *Traitor!*

"Hey, don't look at me." I stood back. "I didn't tell anyone."

"You know her?" DeeBee turned to me.

"No. I just saw her on the shuttle. She was, ah . . . kind of hiding."

"A stowaway!" whistled DeeBee. "I'll bet you're the one who's been messing with the station-drone program!"

The stowaway looked at us as if we'd just dropped out of Alpha Centauri. (That's the closest star to the sun. Well, it's three stars really, but anyway . . .) "Drone program?" she said. "I don't know anything about drones. Shuttles, maybe, but not—"

"Yeah?" DeeBee frowned and punched some buttons on a blinking wall panel. Then she scratched her head, as if she couldn't figure it out. "Hmm. Well. Nothing wrong here. Then who's—"

What was that? The *swish-swoosh* of a door, and maybe footsteps. We saw a silver flash.

"Another wacko station-drone!" I yelled.

First it zoomed in circles, then straight at the stowaway.

I wouldn't have done it. But the stowaway grabbed it with both hands and rode that space puppy all over the hangar. It turned; she turned. It bounced off the wall; so did she. Might have been fun—if the walls had padding. And if she wasn't going backward.

"Let go!" DeeBee and I yelled.

She may have wanted to, but the station-drone had other ideas.

"Ha-ha-ha SNORT!" laughed the drone.

Maybe it was because she was a karate expert. But, finally, the stowaway managed to turn her drone around so she was riding behind it, in control. When it flew close to a work table, she jammed it over to the right.

*Ker-smash!*

Have you seen someone drop a pumpkin before? Think of a pumpkin stuffed full of circuits and wires and switches and blinking stuff, all over the floor.

The poor drone gasped one last time. "Ha . . . ha . . . haaaahhhh."

Then it died, I guess, if that's what drones do. Went offline, maybe. The lights stopped blinking, and the arms went limp, like soggy noodles.

DeeBee drifted a little closer to check it out. She poked at it, but nothing happened. "Look what you did," she whispered.

"I'm sorry." The stowaway stared at the mess. She *did* look sorry. In fact, she looked like she was going to cry. "I thought it was going to hurt us."

Call me a sucker, but I felt sorry for her.

"So turn me in, or do whatever you have to do," she said.

"It wasn't your fault," I blurted.

They both looked at me, as if all of a sudden I was in charge. Okay, so my dad was the new security guy. But what did I know about taking care of stowaways?

"We've got bigger problems," I told them. If they wanted me to be the leader, I could be the leader. "I mean, we didn't fix any drone, here. We can keep trying. But why don't we get you something to eat first? Then we can figure out what to do with you—whoever you are."

# 7 Space Snob   * * *

The stowaway said her name was Miko Sato, short for *Kumiko*. She had come from Moon Colony T-1 and didn't have any parents. She pronounced her name "MEEK-oh," in case you're wondering, the Japanese way. And as I listened to the way she told her story, I didn't think she was lying.

She was hungry, too, so getting something to eat was a good plan. I was hungry myself. You get that way racing around a space station.

"Keep an eye out for wild drones," I told DeeBee and Miko, but I really didn't have to. They were watching both ways as we walked down the hallway. DeeBee ahead of us, Miko behind.

I felt my interface shake. *Deep-doop*, it chimed. Someone was trying to call me. A moment later, I was talking to a holo-picture of my mom, hovering right over my wrist.

"How's your exploring coming, Lamar?"

"Pretty good," I told her.

"Staying out of trouble?"

"Uh . . ."

"Are you making any friends yet?"

"Sure, Mom. I've already bumped into a couple of people."

"I knew you would. But I forgot to tell you that your father and I need you back at the apartments. There's a welcome party in the big room for all the new people."

"Ohh," I groaned. BOR-ing. "Now?"

"They're serving real Jupiter ice cream."

"Not digital food copier stuff?"

"You heard me."

"I'm there!"

QUESTION 04:

So are you finally going to tell us what a digital food copier is?

**ANSWER 04:**

Okay, okay. I guess now's a good time. A digital food copier, or DFC, does just what its name says. Any food you put in, it scans and stores in its computer. When you want it again, just call up the code, and there you go—a digital copy, as many as you want!

**QUESTION 05:**

Just like that?

**ANSWER 05:**

Just like that. Only they're still working on the program, and sometimes burritos taste like broccoli, or spaghetti tastes like Spam. Yuk! On the other hand, there's Jupiter ice cream!

**QUESTION 06:**

From Jupiter?

Answer 06:

Yeah. I'll tell you about it later.

So as I was saying, we had to go over to the apartments, and DeeBee showed us a short-cut through a tunnel where they stored drone parts.

It turned out to be a big mistake.

I almost ran into DeeBee when she stopped.

"Well," said a hollow voice. "It's DeeBee and her new *friends*."

Whoever it was sounded like he was talking through a tube, or an awfully big nose.

DeeBee frowned and held back.

We could turn around, but there was no other way out. A tall person in shiny black overalls with a built-in silver helmet and visor blocked our way. I couldn't see his face behind the glass mask.

"Aren't you going to introduce me, Daphne?" he asked.

"The guy with the mask is Vladimir Chekhov," DeeBee told us with a wave of her hand. "His father is the station commander and president of

Ruski Deep Space, which—"

"Which owns the station." Vladimir flipped up his mask. Wild blond hair and a pair of big ears popped out from behind it. He was smiling. "My friends call me Mir."

"Right, well, *Vladimir*, this is everybody else. Everybody else, this is Vladimir."

*Nice introduction, DeeBee.* She said it "VLAD-ih-meer," and I whispered it a couple of times, really quietly, just to practice.

But Vladimir didn't seem to mind the odd intro. We stood there for a moment. He looked at me; I looked at him. He scratched his nose, as if he was trying to remember something.

I let him wonder.

Didn't he recognize me? Because I sure recognized *him*, even with his suit on. This was the guy who was going to meet me and beat me, or greet me and mistreat me, shake me and bake me. . . . You remember how mad he looked when I snooped on his holo-channel.

"How do you like the new zipsuit my dad bought me?" Vladimir finally asked. He held up his arm, and I could see a tiny row of blaster boosters above his elbow. "It cost a fortune."

So *that's* what it was. Any other time, I would have died to see a zipsuit in action. Or maybe even try one on. *Poosh!* You're flying across space. *Zip!* Faster than a J-4 shuttle. Zipsuits were *very* expensive. And *very* awesome.

"I'd like to see it," Miko piped up. Didn't she understand who this guy was? Didn't she know she was still a stowaway? Didn't she know what could happen to her?

"I don't think so." I tried to stop her, but it was too late. So we watched Vladimir zip from one side of the room to the other. The whole time, he bragged about all the other expensive things his father bought for him, like his interspace wrist interface and his personal drone. Then he told us about their trips to the moon and, of course, his famous relatives. What a show-off.

"My great-great-great-great-great-great-grand-father was the first man to orbit the earth," he told us. (Count 'em yourself—six "greats.") Was he waiting for people to ooh and ahh, or clap?

"Uh, I've heard this story before," said DeeBee. "Gotta go."

"Wait a minute. . . ." He looked at me again.

*Uh-oh. Here it comes.* Vladimir's brain had finally caught up with his blasters. I was beginning to think maybe he wasn't tops in the gifted program. But he looked at me again and kind of smiled.

"We've met before," he said. "Or perhaps you don't remember."

"I remember."

"Well, I just wanted you to know I'm planning an extra-special welcome for you."

"Look, I said I was sorry for snooping on the wrong channels. I was just getting used to my interface."

"Sure you were."

Vladimir grinned again and left.

Well, I couldn't worry about him too much. Not now, anyway. The Jupiter ice cream was waiting for us.

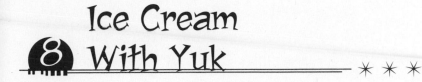

# Ice Cream
# With Yuk

"And so, we welcome you to a brave new frontier, blah blah blah . . ."

I was trying to listen to what tall, dark-haired Station Commander Chekhov was saying. I really was. But you know how it gets when adults go on and on.

So I watched the drones, who were bringing plates of food to each of the levi-tables set up in the assembly hall. There were maybe twenty-five of us new people, with only a few kids. All of us were brought in to get the new station going. Miko blended right in.

QUESTION 07:

Hang on. What are levi-tables? Like the blue jeans?

Answer 07:

Wrong-o. Remember that the *lev* in *mag-lev* stands for levitation? Same thing here. Levi-tables are tables that float off the ground a few feet. They're pretty cool, actually—not like the clunky tables on Earth that rest on legs.

So we were waiting for the ice cream when DeeBee whispered something in my ear.

"I'm going to make my own drone," she told me. "Only better than one of these. And better than Vladimir's."

"Really?" I was interested.

DeeBee nodded. "I figured out a design the other day with some spare parts. Want to help?"

"Would I? Is Mars red?" My stomach rumbled, and my mom looked at me as if I should have been able to help it. Especially with the Jupiter ice cream to come.

Question 08:

You promised to explain—

Answer 08:

Oh yeah. So I did. Jupiter ice cream is made from the ice crystals from Europa, Jupiter's ice moon. (Jupiter has four moons, by the way.) It tastes the best—way better than other ice creams. You can always tell Jupiter ice cream, because it's purple and kind of see-through.

I was still thinking of Jupiter ice cream when everybody clapped. The station commander had finished talking.

"And now, our special treat." A woman floated up so everyone could see her better. She wore a mag-lev belt. "Jupiter ice cream!"

This was going to be good, and I looked for the drones to put the bowls down.

"These things aren't going to start singing about hairbrushes again, are they?" I asked, and the people around me laughed.

"Let's hope not," said my dad. He took one of the dishes and passed it to my mom.

Actually, the drones were behaving themselves. For now. And who knows, maybe that tech in the hallway was right. Maybe it was just a glitch in the program. But I still had a bad feeling.

"Do you sing?" I asked the drone that brought my plate. A green light blinked on the side of the polished silver ball, as if it were thinking about my question.

DeeBee looked up from her bowl, too. Another meltdown?

"I am a 61-40 station-drone," the drone finally answered. "My purpose is to serve the crew of the *CLEO*-7. I am not programmed to sing."

No "groovies" or "ha-ha-ha-ha SNORTs" this time. Good.

The drone squirted a dollop of sauce on top of my ice cream, and after a quick prayer of thanks, I dug in.

I was expecting the sweet, Jupiter ice taste. But my tongue sizzled and my lips quivered. My cheeks puffed out, and my ears steamed. My mouth had been attacked by . . .

"Pit-TOOO!" DeeBee spit out her ice cream.

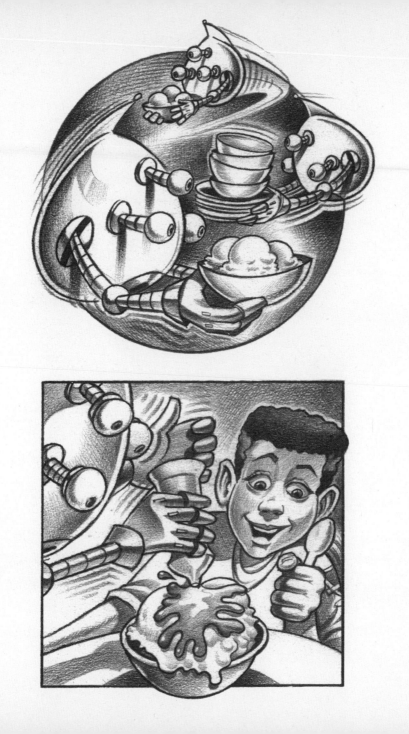

She fell over backward, rolled to her feet, and ran.

An older woman across the table from her screamed and wiped her face.

"Get me a drink!" yelled someone else. "A drink!"

We weren't the only ones having big problems.

"Oh dear!" My mom, Mrs. Manners, looked like she was going to lose it. Her face turned as green as Venus cheese.

"What *is* this?" I asked the nearest drone.

"Would you like more?" it asked, coming up with his spray can.

"No way!" I put up my hands. "Just tell me what it is."

"I have been programmed to provide you with the finest Jupiter ice cream, topped with Mercury hot sauce."

"Mercury hot—" I finished my second gulp of water just in time to hear someone leaving the room, choking. At first I thought it was another one of us. But the choking sounded more like laugh-choking than hot-sauce-choking. And the voice sounded familiar. The door *swish-swooshed* behind him.

"Are you thinking what I'm thinking?" DeeBee came up to me. Miko was right behind her.

I nodded and finished my second glass of water before I stood up. There was only one thing to do.

"I think we need to go see what Vladimir is up to," I told her.

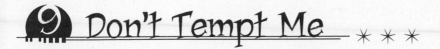

# ⑨ Don't Tempt Me  ✳ ✳ ✳

For the first time, I told DeeBee what I had seen on my wrist interface. Remember Vladimir's laughing and saying "Nobody will ever find out"?

I still didn't know what he meant. But I wanted to find out, more than ever.

First we checked the gardens. No Vladimir. Next the labs, the repair center, even the apartments.

Where else could he be?

"I say let's go back to the hub," said DeeBee. We had only made it halfway there when Tag caught up to us. Or ran into us. Or . . . flew into us.

"Whoop-woo!" he squealed as he zipped by. He was wearing Vladimir's zipsuit!

"You come here, Theodore!" His sister grabbed at his arm, and they spun around.

"You're a good dancer," said Tag. They dragged to a stop after three good swirls. Made me dizzy to watch.

DeeBee made him take the suit off. "Where did you get that?" she demanded.

"Found it in the locker room. Vladimir left his locker unlocked. Finders, keepers, losers—"

"That's not the way it works," DeeBee cut in.

"I know! Let's rearrange all the thrusters for him. Make him go backward." Tag began to fiddle with one of the arms, but DeeBee yanked it away.

"Tag!" she scolded him. "This isn't ours, even if it does belong to . . . *him*."

"Couldn't we just cut the arms off and put it back in the locker?" Tag was getting worse all the time. "That would teach him a *nossel*."

*Nossel?* Oh, right. He meant *lesson*.

"Don't tempt me." DeeBee grinned.

"You keep looking for Vladimir," I told them. "And I'll take care of this."

So I helped Tag get out of the suit and told them I'd put it back where it belonged. We still had to talk to Vladimir about his nasty tricks.

"We'll meet you at the hub," DeeBee told me as she left with Miko and Tag to keep searching for Vladimir.

I nodded, but I couldn't make myself move after they left. Here I was, holding a real zillion-dollar zipsuit. What would it hurt just to look at it?

I looked at it.

And wasn't Vladimir about my size? *I bet he wouldn't mind if I just . . .*

The zipsuit fit really well. Almost perfectly. I wondered how to steer the blaster. Right, left, and . . . for-waaaard!

*Whoosh!* Vladimir wasn't kidding about how fast the suit could travel. *Engage mag-lev, and I'm off the ground.* I flew down to the end of the hall, sending a couple of techs to the wall. A neat one-eighty turned me straight back the way I'd come. This was cooking! Only, how to stop?

Pretty soon I blew right by the other AstroKids.

"I can't stooooop!" I yelled.

Miko nearly flipped.

"Buzz!" cried DeeBee. "What are you—"

"Meet . . . you . . . in . . . the . . . hub!"

Easy for me to say. I was almost there. They were five or ten minutes behind me. And the big set of double doors straight ahead was . . . open!

"Yes!" I told myself and aimed for the doors.

Bad idea. Once I blasted into shuttle hangar 02—the hub—I was almost weightless. The doors swooshed closed behind me, barely knocking my left foot. I spun into the hangar, doing great tumbles and three-sixties.

*Whew.* Good thing no one saw me. Everyone must have been out to lunch. Or maybe they were still at the welcome party. At least, that's what I thought—until I bounced face-first into the front window of the shuttle.

The pilot's window. About a foot away from my nose, on the other side of the glass, was the most red-faced kid I'd ever seen. Vladimir Chekhov was pounding on the inside of the window.

He was going ballistic, pointing at me.

Actually, he was making strangling motions with his hands.

He was not happy.

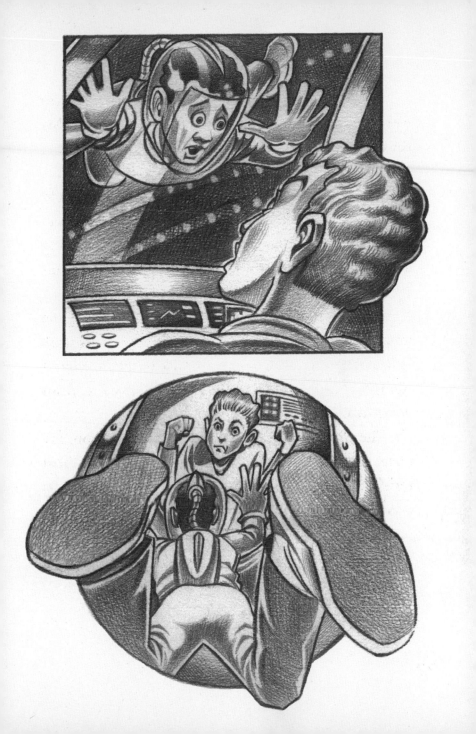

# 10 Blaster Burglar * * *

If I'd been smart, I would have turned around right there. I could have hit the red Blaster button on the belt and whooshed back down the hallway the way I'd come. But I hadn't done too well at whooshing the first time. I would have a couple of bruises from *that* whoosh.

And, besides, this looked bad. I needed to explain to Vladimir that I wasn't really stealing his zipsuit.

"Oh yeah? Well, it sure looked like it." His face wasn't quite as red a few minutes later when I'd told him what had happened. He leaned back in the shuttle-pilot's chair.

"Listen, I'm really sorry," I told him again. "I shouldn't have tried it on. I was going to bring it back to your locker. But I just about blasted myself through the ceiling trying."

Vladimir must have thought that was funny. I started to take the zipsuit off, but he slapped me on the back and laughed.

"I would have liked to see you fly through the ceiling," he said. "That would have been funny."

Funny, as in ha-ha? I wasn't sure. At least Vladimir didn't look ready to shake and bake me anymore.

"I'll show you how to steer," he said. "It takes practice."

Okay. But by that time, I was wondering something else. See, we were standing behind the controls of an expensive space shuttle. I wondered what kind of trouble we were in for just being there.

"Don't worry. I come up here all the time," he bragged. "In fact . . ." He smiled again, like he was about to tell a secret.

"Your friend DeeBee thinks she knows everything," he said. "But if she's so smart, she would know how I control things from right here in the shuttle."

DeeBee and the others should have been there by that time. I checked. Not yet.

"What do you do up here?" I asked.

"See this?" Vladimir walked over to an on-board computer. "All I have to do is link the controls to the communicator. So this computer talks to the drone control computer, and . . ."

"So *that's* how you made the drones go crazy!" I finally got it.

He just smiled and nodded, like he was proud of himself. Well, okay, it must have been pretty tricky for him to figure it out. But this was one sick mind.

"And how did you like the hot sauce I made for you? I promised you'd get a good welcome."

"You did that, too?" I was afraid of what else.

"Didn't you think it was funny?"

How was I supposed to answer that?

Vladimir's grin slipped away. "You're not going to tell my father, are you?" he asked.

I looked at him and saw something new in his eyes. This guy wasn't a bully, I could tell. For the first time, he was looking a little scared. The bragging, the wild jokes . . . maybe he was just trying to get attention, to get people to notice him.

"You stop messing with the drones, and I won't tell," I said. "But my friends . . ."

. . . were just stumbling into the shuttle bay. DeeBee in front, Miko next, and Tag tagging along. They looked around. At first, they didn't see us up in the shuttle.

"Shh!" Vladimir held a finger to his lips. "I'll lock the door behind them so nobody follows them."

"You can do that from here?"

"Of course." Vladimir started to press some buttons on the shuttle controls. The lights blinked, and the side door to the *shuttle* slammed shut.

"Whoops." Vladimir hit some more buttons, and an alarm buzzer sounded. "Double whoops!"

Everybody down on the floor below us looked up. DeeBee waved.

Then they heard the same voice over the loud-speakers that we did. "THIRTY SECONDS TO LAUNCH. CLEAR THE SHUTTLE BAY!"

"Launch?" I panicked. "What did you do?"

Vladimir bit his lip, looked around us, and

started punching every button in sight. "I, uh, I thought . . ."

"TWENTY SECONDS."

"Oh, great." I couldn't get the side door open to get out. Vladimir couldn't do anything to stop the launch. DeeBee, Miko, and Tag could only run back the way they came. They didn't want to get sucked out into space as the big doors opened, and I sure couldn't blame them.

"TEN SECONDS. NINE . . ."

"Is it really going to launch?" I knew the answer to my question.

Vladimir just kept punching buttons. I sat down in the co-pilot's chair and locked on the safety field that would keep me in the seat.

"THREE, TWO, ONE . . ."

# 11 Lunar Crunch  ✱ ✱ ✱

Funny how being in big trouble together makes you forget things.

"I don't understand it." Vladimir kept busy by punching buttons. He couldn't keep the moon from getting bigger and bigger in our front windows.

Nice view.

But if we couldn't stop this shuttle . . . I thought of what happened when bugs hit windshields, back on Earth.

We were the bug. The moon was the windshield.

And all the lights were blinking red on the control panel. So were the numbers and touch-panels. No wonder Vladimir didn't know what was going on. I tried to shut off an alarm. "I think this one is—"

"Don't touch it!" Vladimir waved his hand.

"You might break something."

"Okay," I told him. The moon was getting bigger and bigger. "But *we're* going to break if we don't turn around soon."

"I know, I know." Vladimir was sweating like a planetary pig. And if he pulled at his hair any more, he wasn't going to have much left.

Me, I thought it would be a good time to pray. Not just like *Lord, help!* but for Vladimir. Even after what he did, we were in this together. I didn't mind praying for him. But I have to tell you, I was starting to sweat, too.

"You acted like you knew how to run this thing," I said.

He turned a brighter shade of red. "I used the controls only to play jokes on the station. Make the drones do funny things, make doors open and shut when they weren't supposed to. I thought people would think I was funny, but it got kind of . . ."

"Out of hand?"

He nodded. Vladimir rested his face in his hands. I thought I saw tears in his eyes.

"Look, I'm sorry," he told me. "I'm really sorry.

If I could do it over, I would do it differently."

"Easy for you to say now. We're about to flatten ourselves on the moon, and you say you're sorry."

"Well, I am." He looked at his hands, and then I felt really bad for him.

We were quiet for a few seconds.

"I'm sorry, too." I tried to remember what I should be sorry for. Mainly for taking the zipsuit without permission—that was a jerky thing to do. I took off the glove of the suit.

"Could you two quit apologizing and pay attention?"

"Who was that? I thought we were the only ones—"

"Hello-o? Buzz? Down here. Wake up!"

What? A head had popped up from my wrist interface. I hadn't noticed before because it had been covered by the suit. But now I saw the head of DeeBee Ortiz, in living color. She looked great.

"What have you been doing, sitting on your wrist?" she asked, almost yelling. "The whole station is worried about you. What happened?"

I heard another voice, too. Very worried sounding. Someone must have been talking to DeeBee, maybe telling her what to say to us. She nodded and looked back at me.

"The commander wants me to tell you that you're going to crash in less than five minutes if you don't turn around now and fire the forward thrusters."

Vladimir and I looked at each other like two people who are about to die. Because that's the way it felt.

"Do you hear me?" DeeBee asked again. "Buzz, this is serious. We're almost out of interface range."

She was right. Her hologram started to fuzz out. We were almost too far away from the station for it to work.

"Wait a minute!" I yelled at her, as if that would help. "We don't know how to turn the ship around."

"Who's at the controls?" Another face poked into the hologram. The image was getting fuzzy, but I could tell it was Miko.

I unstrapped my interface and handed it to Vladimir.

"Mir? Are you all right?" asked Miko. It was "Mir" now, not Vladimir. She watched his face. Mir seemed more scared than ever.

I looked out the window and knew why. I could see craters and shadows, round igloos, and a bright, domed city.

"Okay, Mir, here's what you do. . . ." I don't know how she knew, but she did. Miko was full of surprises. "On your left—see a group of yellow buttons?"

✳ ✳ ✳

A minute later, I cheered when the shuttle slowly turned around to face the right direction. Now we could see *CLEO-7* again. That was better.

"Now start the thrusters," Miko told Mir.

He nodded and wiped the sweat from his forehead.

"Do you see the button?" asked Miko. "Press it . . . *now!*"

That was the last we heard from Miko or DeeBee or anybody else from the station. We were still sliding backward into the moon. And even though Mir pressed the button Miko had told him to press, nothing happened. He pressed it again and again, then pounded the control panel.

"It won't work!" he cried. "And it's all my fault!"

Mir was right, of course, but I didn't have time to make him feel better. This didn't look good. There was only one more thing to try.

I slipped the glove back on the zipsuit and snapped down the face cover.

"I'm going out there," I said.

*Crazy or not, here I come.*

# 12 Touchdown! ✳ ✳ ✳

I could tell you I was brave and that I did all the right things. Maybe you'd be impressed. Truth is, I couldn't stop sh-sh-shaking as I pushed out through the shuttle air lock. Would this work, or would I be turned into lunar road-kill?

*Whoosh!* My legs floated up behind me, but I held on to an outside handle.

Mir pushed his nose against a side window to see out better.

Too bad I didn't have a communicator in this suit. Old-fashioned hand waving would have to do. I gave Mir a thumbs-up and almost lost my grip.

He waved back before I slid around toward the back of the shuttle, out of Mir's sight.

Okay, I was still alive. Good so far. Then I realized where I was. I don't have enough "wows" and "awesomes" to explain what drifting in space was like.

Ever floated upside-down underwater in a swimming pool? It felt kind of like that, only different.

What was different? For one thing, the humongous black sky was close enough to touch. And stars crowded all around me, like I was swimming in them. I was thinking this was a whole lot better than peeking at the sky through a window, or a view screen.

I was also wishing I could have tried space-walking some other time.

*Take it easy,* I told myself, but who was I kidding? My teeth ch-ch-chattered, and not because I was cold.

"Whoa, whoa, whoa . . ." Next, my visor started to fog up, I was breathing so fast.

I couldn't pinch myself, so I blinked my eyes shut, hard, for just a second. And I held my breath.

Now, I don't want to give you the idea that the

only time I pray is when I'm about to become a space pizza. But by that time, I was praying non-stop. Next thing I knew, I had reached the back end of the shuttle.

*If this doesn't work, Mir,* I thought, *we're toast.*

The idea was to use the zipsuit blasters to push us away from the moon. And I was attached to them, of course.

Thing is, I really didn't know if the blasters would work on a big thing like a shuttle. But there wasn't time for a second shot. It was this, or . . .

*"Oof!"* I wasn't ready for the press of the zip-suit's blasters. They flattened my face against the visor. Against the shuttle. They flattened the rest of my body, too. I couldn't breathe. This was *not* what the blaster suit was for.

But I kept my finger glued to the red Max Thrust button on the side of the suit. And I counted to ten. Then twenty. Then thirty. I could feel the heat of the blasters even through the suit. I would get back home—or melt trying.

✳ ✳ ✳

"Ohh," I sighed and slumped back in the co-pilot's chair. For the first time since getting back inside the shuttle, I took a deep breath and closed my eyes. I tried to relax, wondering what would happen to us. Just ahead, the shuttle-bay doors opened wide. Our shuttle wiggled a bit from side to side, right behind the space tow-scooter.

"You must really hate me." Mir sounded tired, too.

"No, I don't." I kept my eyes shut. Was I bothered? Well, yeah, a little. Okay, *a lot*. But hate?

No.

"I don't hate you, Mir."

"After the way I treated you, and . . ."

"All right, all right. You don't need to keep banging your head into the wall. It's okay."

"No, it's just that—"

"Listen, if it makes you feel any better, it *was* kind of funny when you made the drones start singing those weird songs." I opened one eye to see that he was grinning again.

"Really? Want me to show you how I did it?

Look here. In this computer, there's a way to override—"

"No, no, NO!" I sat up straight and waved my arms in the air. "I've had enough goof-ups to last me ten Pluto years. We don't need any more. Let's just get home, all right?"

So Mir zipped his grin and got serious. It was a good move. By that time, our ship thunked softly against the floor of the shuttle-bay floor. *Home* on *CLEO*-7. The doors opened with a whoosh of air, and we were surrounded by techs. A minute later, they had us outside the shuttle.

"Tell us what happened!" DeeBee's parents were there. So were DeeBee and Tag and Miko . . . all the AstroKids. We had some explaining to do.

"We used Mir's zipsuit to push us back," I said. I pointed at Mir.

"I always knew my boy could do anything!" said Station Commander Chekhov. He slapped Mir on the back with a big smile. "Your quick thinking not only saved this shuttle, my son, but two lives, as well!"

"Your son is a hero!" Someone started clapping.

I winked at Mir. It was up to him to tell the truth.

Mir swallowed hard, then looked back up at his father. I could only imagine what he was thinking.

"It wasn't . . ." he began, and he shook his head. "It wasn't me. It was Buzz."

"Lamar?" That had to be my mom. My parents had made it to the front of the crowd.

Mir was just warming up. "It was all my fault we launched," he confessed. "I was messing around where I shouldn't have been. It was an accident, but still it was my fault. Buzz was the one who pushed us back to safety with the zipsuit. DeeBee and Miko helped us, too, over Buzz's interface."

So that was it. Of course, there was more to it than that, but it would take too long to explain. Actually, I would tell you right now, if I wasn't so pumped up about the next AstroKids adventure. But I *can* tell you that those wacko drones seemed to behave themselves after we got back to the station. Especially after Mir 'fessed up to his dad. That's when I had a feeling Mir might make a pretty good AstroKid . . . once he wasn't grounded anymore.

I figured that would be in another two hundred years or so.

# RealSpace Debrief

\* \* \*

## The AstroKids Guide to Real (and Pretend) Space Stations

The idea for space stations has been around a lot longer than you might guess. Try 1857! That's when a crazy story by Edward Hale appeared in *Atlantic Monthly* magazine. Hale wrote about a huge, hollow brick ball up in space. It's the first known mention of a space outpost.

Fast-forward to 1923, when German scientist Hermann Oberth imagined what he called "space stations." Oberth thought the stations would be needed if people ever wanted to get to the moon or Mars.

People liked Oberth's ideas so much that the Society for Space Travel was formed. One of the members was Wernher von Braun, another German scientist who helped the United States build its first space rockets in the 1940s.

Don't forget pretend space stations. The first ring-shaped stations started showing up in the movies (and even Disney TV shows) during the 1950s. In 1968, the movie *2001* showed a giant ring-shaped station, complete with a Hilton hotel.

History's first real space station was the Soviet Union's *Salyut 1*, launched in April 1971. It was not a ring-shaped station, but a tube shape. After that came the Russian *Mir* station.

The Americans' first try at a space station was in 1973. Three three-man crews orbited the earth in *Skylab* for just over 171 days. They studied the earth, the sun, and zero gravity. *Skylab* crashed in 1979. (Good thing it was empty.)

Now comes the *ISS*, or *International Space Station*. Led by the North American Space Agency (NASA), sixteen countries are working together to build the largest-ever space station. It will have not just lab areas, but also a kitchen and sleeping rooms. It was supposed to be finished by 2003, but . . . no one has ever built a station the size of a city block before. When it's done, expect the station and its solar panels to reflect the sun at night—and look brighter than most stars!

Who will work on the *ISS*? Biologists, chemists, engineers, pilots, lab workers, technicians . . . And, hey, who knows? Maybe *you*!

Want to find out more about space and space stations? Then check out

- "The International Space Station" in *Popular Science* magazine, May 1998.
- "Your Future in Outer Space" in *Breakaway* magazine, May 1997.
- Kidsat (on the Web at *www.kidsat.jpl.nasa .gov*). Actual shuttle-based photos and more for kids.
- Kids' Lunar Base (on the Web at *www.njin.net /dmollica/index.html*). Fun moon stuff.
- Everything Space (on the Web at *www.jsc .nasa.gov/pao/students*). Cool kids' links to everything from shuttle information to the latest on the *International Space Station*.

# And the Coded Message Is . . .

$*$ $*$ $*$

You think this ASTROKIDS adventure is over? Uh-uh! Nope. No way.

Here's the plan: We'll give you the coordinates, you find the words. Write them all on a piece of paper. They form a secret message that has to do with *The Great Galaxy Goof.* If you think you got it right, log on to *www.coolreading.com* and follow the instructions there. You'll receive free ASTRO-KIDS wallpaper for your computer and a sneak peek at the next ASTROKIDS adventure. It's that simple!

WORD 1:
chapter 11, paragraph 10, word 11  _____

WORD 2:
chapter 6, paragraph 3, word 19  _____

WORD 3:
chapter 2, paragraph 10, word 6    _____

WORD 4:
chapter 3, paragraph 1, word 45    _____

WORD 5:
chapter 7, paragraph 9, word 1    _____

WORD 6:
chapter 6, paragraph 37, word 15    _____

WORD 7:
chapter 4, paragraph 3, word 7    _____

WORD 8:
chapter 8, paragraph 1, word 5    _____

WRITE IT ALL HERE:

_____

_____

(Tag says you could look it up yourself in 82:6 ekul.)

# Contact Us

If you have questions for the author or just want to say hi, feel free to contact him at Bethany House Publishers, 11400 Hampshire Avenue South, Minneapolis, MN 55438, United States of America, EARTH. Please include a stamped, self-addressed envelope if you'd like a reply. Or log on to Robert's intergalactic Web site at *www.coolreading.com*.

# Launch
## Countdown

$*$ $*$ $*$

In the second ASTROKIDS adventure, Moon Rock rules! Everybody's pumped up when Zero-G comes to give a concert at the *CLEO*-7 space station. After all, they're only the most awesome band in the universe. The AstroKids are ready to rock.

Everyone except DeeBee and her little brother, Tag, that is. They have to go to a violin recital put on by their visiting cousin, Phil Harmonic. BORing! Even worse, DeeBee's drone project for school has just melted down. Can DeeBee, the station genius, fix things before she . . . flunks?

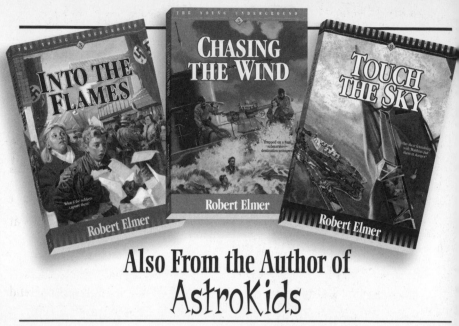

# Also From the Author of
# AstroKids

Boys and girls from all over the country write to Robert Elmer telling him how much they love THE YOUNG UNDERGROUND books—have you read them?

In THE YOUNG UNDERGROUND, eleven-year-old Peter Andersen and his twin sister, Elise, are living in the city of Helsingor, Denmark, during World War II. There are German soldiers everywhere—on the streets, in patrol boats in the harbor, and in fighter planes in the sky. Peter and Elise must help their Jewish friend Henrik and his parents escape to Sweden. But with Nazi boats patrolling the sea, they'll need a miracle to get their friends to safety!

Throughout the series Peter and Elise come face-to-face with guard dogs, arsonists, and spies. Together they rescue a downed British bomber pilot, search for treasure, become trapped on a Nazi submarine, and uncover a plot to assassinate the King of Denmark!

## Read all eight exciting, danger-filled books in THE YOUNG UNDERGROUND!

*A Way Through the Sea*    *Chasing the Wind*

*Beyond the River*    *A Light in the Castle*

*Into the Flames*    *Follow the Star*

*Far From the Storm*    *Touch the Sky*

*Available from your local Christian bookstores or from Bethany House Publishers.*

## The Leader in Christian Fiction!
### BETHANY HOUSE PUBLISHERS

11400 Hampshire Ave. South
Minneapolis, MN 55438
www.bethanyhouse.com

# Take a Trip of the Imagination With

# ADVENTURES DOWN UNDER!

With exciting plots that will take your breath away and interesting glimpses at one of the most fascinating far-off places, Robert Elmer's series ADVENTURES DOWN UNDER spins the globe to deliver you to the rough-and-tumble outback of Australia in the 1860s.

When his father is framed for a crime and sent on the last prison ship to Australia in 1867, Patrick McWaid and his family find passage on another ship and head "down under." Presented with a land of outlaws, riverboats, and high adventure, Patrick finds himself in the midst of a wild land as he and his friends continue the search for Mr. McWaid.

ADVENTURES DOWN UNDER opens a window for you to glimpse a fascinating era and the role that faith played in developing it.

1. Escape to
   Murray River
2. Captive at
   Kangaroo Springs
3. Rescue at
   Boomerang Bend
4. Dingo Creek Challenge
5. Race to Wallaby Bay
6. Firestorm at
   Kookaburra Station
7. Koala Beach Outbreak
8. Panic at Emu Flat

## The Leader in Christian Fiction!
### BETHANY HOUSE PUBLISHERS

11400 Hampshire Ave. South
Minneapolis, MN 55438
www.bethanyhouse.com

Available from your nearest Christian bookstore (800) 991-7747 or from Bethany House Publishers.

# Series for Young Readers*
# From Bethany House Publishers

### THE ADVENTURES OF CALLIE ANN
*by Shannon Mason Leppard*

Readers will giggle their way through the true-to-life escapades of Callie Ann Davies and her many North Carolina friends.

### ASTROKIDS™
*by Robert Elmer*

Space scooters? Floating robots? Jupiter ice cream? Blast into the future for out-of-this-world, zero-gravity fun with the AstroKids on space station *CLEO-7*.

### BACKPACK MYSTERIES
*by Mary Carpenter Reid*

This excitement-filled mystery series follows the mishaps and adventures of Steff and Paulie Larson as they strive to help often-eccentric relatives crack their toughest cases.

### THE CUL-DE-SAC KIDS
*by Beverly Lewis*

Each story in this lighthearted series features the hilarious antics and predicaments of nine endearing boys and girls who live on Blossom Hill Lane.

### JANETTE OKE'S ANIMAL FRIENDS
*by Janette Oke*

Endearing creatures from the farm, forest, and zoo discover their place in God's world through various struggles, mishaps, and adventures.

### RUBY SLIPPERS SCHOOL
*by Stacy Towle Morgan*

Join the fun as home-schoolers Hope and Annie Brown visit fascinating countries and meet inspiring Christians from around the world!

### THREE COUSINS DETECTIVE CLUB®
*by Elspeth Campbell Murphy*

Famous detective cousins Timothy, Titus, and Sarah-Jane learn compelling Scripture-based truths while finding—and solving—intriguing mysteries.

*(ages 7–10)

# Series for Middle Graders* From BHP

### ADVENTURES DOWN UNDER · by Robert Elmer
When Patrick McWaid's father is unjustly sent to Australia as a prisoner in 1867, the rest of the family follows, uncovering action-packed mystery along the way.

### ADVENTURES OF THE NORTHWOODS · by Lois Walfrid Johnson
Kate O'Connell and her stepbrother Anders encounter mystery and adventure in northwest Wisconsin near the turn of the century.

### AN AMERICAN ADVENTURE SERIES · by Lee Roddy
Hildy Corrigan and her family must overcome danger and hardship during the Great Depression as they search for a "forever home."

### BLOODHOUNDS, INC. · by Bill Myers
Hilarious, hair-raising suspense follows brother-and-sister detectives Sean and Melissa Hunter in these madcap mysteries with a message.

### GIRLS ONLY! · by Beverly Lewis
Four talented young athletes become fast friends as together they pursue their Olympic dreams.

### MANDIE BOOKS · by Lois Gladys Leppard
With over five million sold, the turn-of-the-century adventures of Mandie and her many friends will keep readers eager for more.

### PROMISE OF ZION · by Robert Elmer
Following WWII, thirteen-year-old Dov Zalinsky leaves for Palestine—the one place he may still find his parents—and meets the adventurous Emily Parkinson. Together they experience the dangers of life in the Holy Land.

### THE RIVERBOAT ADVENTURES · by Lois Walfrid Johnson
Libby Norstad and her friend Caleb face the challenges and risks of working with the Underground Railroad during the mid–1800s.

### TRAILBLAZER BOOKS · by Dave and Neta Jackson
Follow the exciting lives of real-life Christian heroes through the eyes of child characters as they share their faith with others around the world.

### THE TWELVE CANDLES CLUB · by Elaine L. Schulte
When four twelve-year-old girls set up a business of odd jobs and baby-sitting, they uncover wacky adventures and hilarious surprises.

### THE YOUNG UNDERGROUND · by Robert Elmer
Peter and Elise Andersen's plots to protect their friends and themselves from Nazi soldiers in World War II Denmark guarantee fast-paced action and suspenseful reads.

*(ages 8–13)